Wishker

Heather Pindar Sarah Jennings

For Madge, the rufty-tufty roaming cat
with very large whiskers.
- HP

For my own little Wishker
and beloved studio companion.
- SJ

When Mirabel wanted something,
the answer always seemed to be the same.

"Please can my friends come for a sleepover?" "No."

"Can I have a pet monkey?"

"NO!"

"Can I play in your bedroom, Jim?"

"No! NO WAY. NOT EVER."

"It's not fair! Everyone always says NO."

"Is that so? Purrr-haps I can help?" said a quiet voice.

Mirabel jumped. A cat was sitting beside her!

"Hello, who are you?" asked Mirabel.
"My name is Wishker. I'm just a
rufty-tufty roaming cat, but I can do magic..."

"...And I will give you three wishes.
Use each whisker to make a wish."

Mirabel knew exactly what to wish for;

"I wish that everyone says YES to me!"

Whoosh

Had Mirabel's wish really come true? Time to find out!

"Gran," said Mirabel, "can we have ice cream for breakfast, lunch and tea?"

"Yes," said Gran. "Now you're talking!"

"Mum, can all my friends come to stay? For ever?"

"Yes of course, what a lovely idea!"
said Mum.

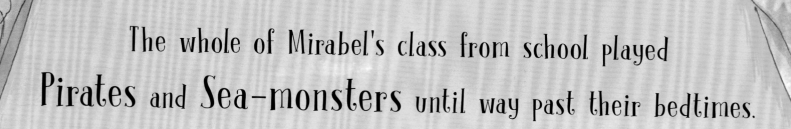

The whole of Mirabel's class from school played
Pirates and Sea-monsters until way past their bedtimes.

The next morning Mirabel rang the **circus**.

"I want **clowns** please,
fire-eaters and some **acrobats**."

"Yes, certainly, we'll come straight away,"
said the ringmaster. And they did.

Then of course the zoo said
YES to the hippo...

...two elephants, three giraffes, four zebras, ten parrots

and lots of monkeys.

Oh, and a lion.

But when a small house is **squashed** full of friends, animals and circus people, things don't always go to plan...

There was non-stop neighing and stamping, squawking and roaring.

There were muddy hoof-prints everywhere and some very stinky smells.

And as for having a bath, or eating anything
EXCEPT ice cream, or even just sleeping...

...it was **impossible**.

"This isn't FUN anymore!

I wish everything was NORMAL again!"

In a flash the house looked spick and span and cosy again.
"You have one wish left," said a quiet voice.

"No, please take back the last whisker," said Mirabel. "I'm not very good at magic wishes but there is one thing I want to ask..."

"Please can this **rufty-tufty roaming** cat live with us?" asked Mirabel.

"What?" said Gran, "Just this little cat here?
No lions or monkeys?"
"Yes," said Mirabel.

"Just ONE cat?" said Mum.
"Well in that case the answer is...

...YES!"

"That's not fair!" said Jim. "Mirabel's got a pet,
but I never get anything I ask for.
Everyone always says NO!"

"Is that so?" said Wishker in his quiet voice, "Well I happen to have this **one spare magic** whisker. You can have it...

...Use it to make a **wish.**"

The End

Wishker

An original concept by author Heather Pindar

© Heather Pindar

Illustrated by Sarah Jennings

MAVERICK ARTS PUBLISHING LTD

Studio 3A, City Business Centre, 6 Brighton Road, Horsham, West Sussex, RH13 5BB

© Maverick Arts Publishing Limited October 2016 +44 (0)1403 256941

Published May 2017

A CIP catalogue record for this book is available at the British Library.

ISBN 978-1-84886-244-9

Maverick
arts publishing
www.maverickbooks.co.uk